Lydia Dabcovich

DUCKS FLY

DUTTON CHILDREN'S BOOKS   NEW YORK

Copyright © 1990 by Lydia Dabcovich

Library of Congress Cataloging-in-Publication Data
Dabcovich, Lydia.
  Ducks fly/Lydia Dabcovich.—1st ed.
    p.   cm.
  Summary: While his brothers and sisters learn to
fly, one little duck stays behind—but is finally
surprised into trying his wings.
  ISBN 0-525-44586-2
  1. Ducks—Juvenile fiction.   [1. Ducks—Fiction.
2. Flight—Fiction.]   I. Title.   89-38716
PZ10.3.D17Du 1990   CIP
[E]—dc20   AC

Published in the United States by
Dutton Children's Books,
a division of Penguin Books USA Inc.

Published simultaneously in Canada by
Fitzhenry & Whiteside Limited, Toronto

Editor: Ann Durell

Printed in Hong Kong by South China Printing Co.
First Edition   10 9 8 7 6 5 4 3 2 1

for Milan, whose idea this was,
and for Wendy, who inspired it

Ducks fly

way up high–

and back again.

"Quack, quack, quack!"

Ducks fly–

all but one . . .

Swim, paddle, float

past forests and fields,
and then–

"Quack, quack!"

Flap,   flap,

flap,

flap–

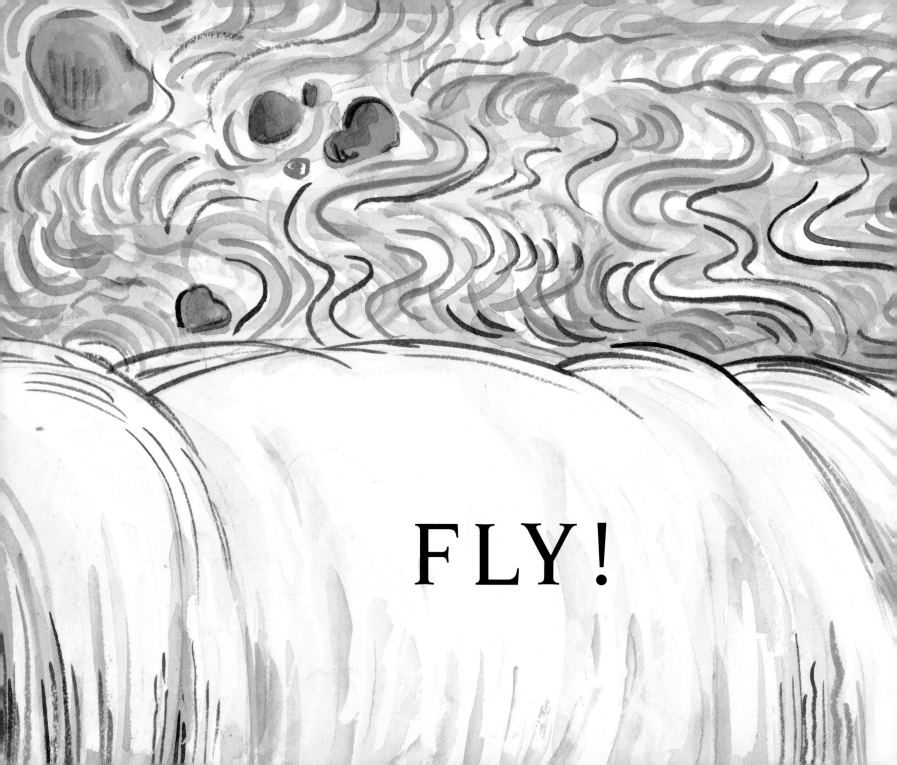

FLY!

Way up high–
over forests and fields.

"Quack! Quack!"

Ducks fly.